For Sohana,
my beautiful, clever daughter, who smiles through her pain
but never stops hoping to fly in the future—S. C.

Text © 2019 Sharmila Collins
Illustrations © 2019 Carolina Rabei

Published in Great Britain in 2019 by Otter-Barry Books, Little Orchard, Burley Gate, Herefordshire, HR1 3QS. www.otterbarrybooks.com.

Published in the United States of America in 2020 by Flyaway Books, 100 Witherspoon Street, Louisville, Kentucky 40202-1396.
Online at www.flyawaybooks.com.

20 21 22 23 24 25 26 27 28 29–10 9 8 7 6 5 4 3 2 1

Book design by Allison Taylor
Text set in Simplicité

Library of Congress Control Number: 2019034261

PRINTED IN CHINA

Most Flyaway Books are available at special quantity discounts when purchased in bulk by corporations, organizations, and special-interest groups. For more information, please e-mail SpecialSales@flyawaybooks.com.

Binkle's Time to Fly

SHARMILA COLLINS

Illustrated by
CAROLINA RABEI

Binkle was waiting.

First he was an egg.

Then he was a hungry caterpillar.

And then he was in a cocoon.

But what he really wanted to be was a butterfly, with big and beautiful wings.

At last the day came!
The sun was shining,
and its warmth gave Binkle strength.

He pushed and pushed . . .

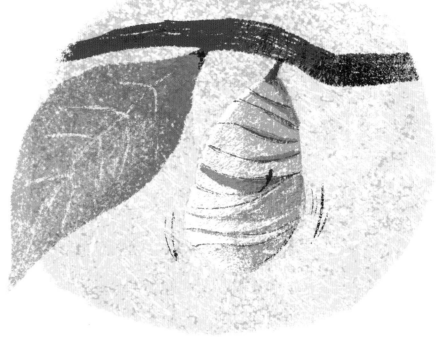

and cracked his cocoon . . .

and out he came to say
"Hello!" to the world.

But . . .

when Binkle opened his wings,
they didn't work.

They were weak and pale, silvery, wispy, and unfinished.
They had a wing shape and a wing frame
but only a few strands of wing
and holes instead of color.
And they would not and could not let him fly.

Binkle's heart was full of sorrow
and disappointed dreams.
His fragile wings shimmered
in the pale moonlight.
What could he do?

He slunk away and hid under a leaf,

unhappy at being different.

Two crows came along to see if Binkle was worth eating,
but they stared and laughed at him instead.

"There isn't much to eat on him," they cawed,
and they flew away.

But then two butterflies, who had been caterpillars with Binkle, came to find him.

"We will help you," they said.

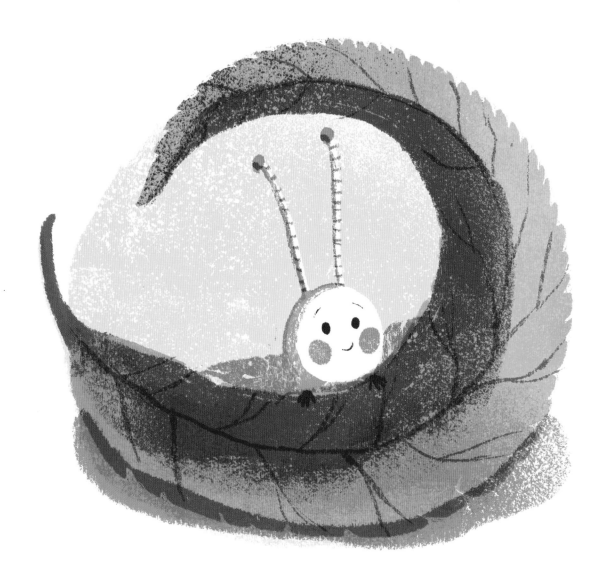

Binkle crept out from behind his leaf.
How could they help?

First the butterflies found a friendly bird
to carry Binkle to the zoo.

There they found silkworms
munching on mulberry leaves

and spiders busily making their webs.

"Please, will you help us?" the butterflies asked.

The silkworms and spiders were glad to help.
The silkworms spun fine silver silk thread,
and the spiders wove the threads
into Binkle's wings to make them strong.
Then they asked the bees to inject them with all
the colors of the rainbow,
in wild and intricate patterns.

Binkle stayed very still as the butterflies fluttered above.
At last the work was finished,
and the silkworms, spiders, and bees admired their handiwork.
"It's amazing what we can do if we all work together!"
they said to one another.

But Binkle still had his eyes shut.

"Open your wings, Binkle!"
they all called.
Binkle took a deep breath.
Very, very slowly, he opened his wings.
His heart was full of hope and longing.
His wings felt heavier and stronger,
as if they might let him fly.
Binkle opened his eyes.

The wings were magnificent!
They were strong!
There were no holes,
just woven silk threads
with bold and beautiful colors.

"I am different from all other butterflies,
and I always will be," said Binkle.
"But I don't care—all I want to do is fly."

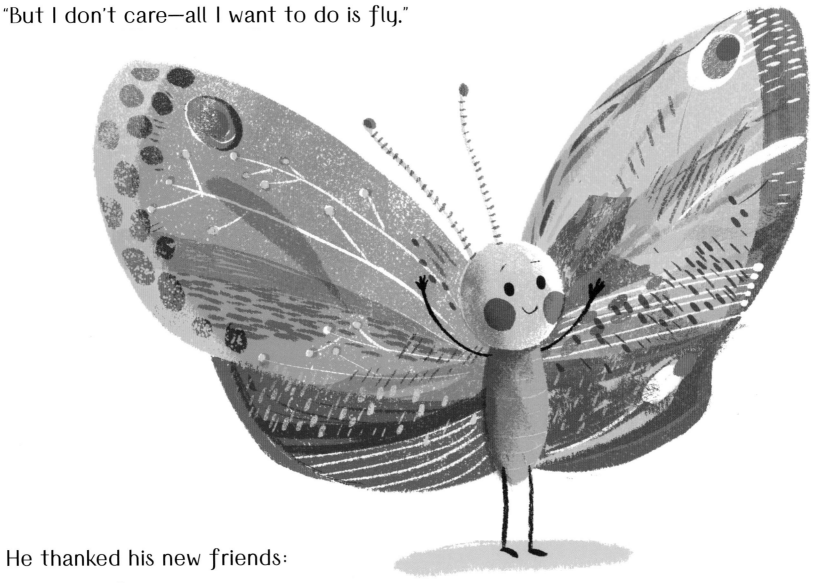

He thanked his new friends:
the butterflies, the bird,
the silkworms, the spiders, and the bees.

The butterflies rose into the air
and fluttered above him.
"Come on, Binkle," they called.

"It's time to fly!"

Binkle tested his wings, opening and closing them carefully,
once, twice, three times.
Then, with the silver in his wings glinting in the sun,
Binkle rose up into the air

and FLEW
to join his friends.

A Note from the Author

This is a story about hope—and flying is about freedom. Every day, everywhere, children come into the world with conditions that make their lives more challenging. Some are medical: their bodies don't work as designed. Some are emotional: they enter an inhospitable environment. Most difficulties are well outside the child's control. Yet hope blooms when a community comes around that child, offering support and creative solutions that can make life a bit easier and more beautiful, even if the condition remains.

My daughter, Sohana, has severe recessive dystrophic epidermolysis bullosa (EB), an incurable skin condition that causes blistering, skin loss, and malignant skin cancer, in severe types. There is no cure as yet, and 500,000 people worldwide live with this disease. Children with EB are said to have skin as fragile as a butterfly's wings and are often called butterfly children. Their skin is fragile, but they are not. They have wounds dressed and blisters pricked every day. They have difficulty eating because of mouth and throat blisters and difficulty walking because of blistering on their legs and feet, and sometimes they cannot see because of blisters on their eyes. They face these great difficulties with strength, humor, and spirit, rising to the challenges of physical pain and social isolation without losing hope that one day they will be free. My daughter's positive spirit and resilience fill me with admiration. Watching and participating in her pain inspired the founding of a charity, Cure EB, which funds research and clinical trials in search of effective treatments that may one day lead to a cure.

Whatever may keep you or a child you know from flying, perhaps Binkle will remind you, as he does Sohana, that there is hope when we gather around each other to offer support, creativity, and beauty.

All author royalties from this book
will go toward Cure EB, which you can
learn more about at www.cure-eb.org.